The Princess and the Dragons

With special thanks to ML

~*AD*

STRIPES PUBLISHING
An imprint of Little Tiger Press
1 The Coda Centre, 189 Munster Road,
London SW6 6AW

A paperback original
First published in Great Britain in 2012

ISBN: 978-1-84715-187-2

A CIP catalogue record for this book is available from the British Library.

Printed and bound in the UK.

2 4 6 8 10 9 7 5 3 1

The Magic Secrets Box

The Princess and the Dragons

Sue Mongredien

Stripes

Azure Skies
The Land of Eight Kingdoms
Silver City
Sunny Meadows
Emerald Seas

Misty Mountains
White Frost
Evergreen Forest
Golden Spires

Chapter One

Megan Andrews couldn't stop smiling. She was so excited! Today she was going to her first ever riding lesson at the local stables, and she'd been looking forward to it for weeks.

"Come on, darling, time to go!" her mum called from downstairs.

"Coming!" Megan shouted back. But just as she was about to hurry out of her room, a noise stopped her in her tracks. A delicate, tinkling melody had begun to play from her music box, and Megan saw

that the fairy figure within it was twirling around, her pretty dress glittering in the sunlight.

A thrill rushed through Megan as she ran over to her chest of drawers. The Fairy Queen was coming back to life!

It had been the biggest surprise ever, discovering that the broken old music box she'd bought from a second-hand shop contained such an amazing secret. The Fairy Queen from the Land of Eight Kingdoms was trapped inside, imprisoned there by a spell from the wicked enchanter Sorcero!

According to the Fairy Queen, she would only be freed if Megan could befriend and help someone in all eight of the magical kingdoms. So far Megan had been to three of them, helping a ballerina,

a mermaid and a woodsprite along the way. But there were still five kingdoms left to visit before the Fairy Queen could even hope to go home…

"Hello," Megan said excitedly.

The Fairy Queen stopped spinning and smiled up at Megan. "Hello there," she said, giving her right arm a little shake. Her body had been stiff and lifeless when Megan first met her, but now, thanks to Megan's adventures, the Fairy Queen could move her head and the whole of her right arm again. Slowly but surely, she was returning to her usual self and becoming stronger. "That's better," she said. "How long have I been away?"

"A whole week," Megan replied. "I was starting to get worried. I'm glad you're all right."

"I'm fine," the Fairy Queen said. "Although I fear I have been awoken because Sorcero has done something terrible again. Shall we take a look in the magic mirror?"

"Yes," Megan answered eagerly, just as another shout came from downstairs.

"Megan! What are you doing?" her mum called.

"Two minutes!" Megan yelled back. There was no way she could leave the Fairy Queen now. Not when the chance of another amazing adventure in the Land of Eight Kingdoms lay ahead! Besides, once she was actually in the land, time would stop in the human world so that she could go there and back in the blink of an eye.

"If you're ready, then touch the tip of

my wand, and I can use its magic to make a wish," the Fairy Queen said.

Megan obediently touched the wand and felt it tremble, as if ready to unleash a stream of magic.

"Show us Sorcero!" the Fairy Queen commanded.

A swirl of golden sparkles whirled around the mirror in the lid of the music box, fizzing and crackling with dazzling magical light.

As the sparkles faded, an image appeared in the mirror and Megan shuddered to see a tall, craggy-faced man whose dark eyes glittered with menace. Sorcero was standing in a rocky valley dotted with red boulders, his long black cloak swirling around him in the wind as he shouted a string of strange words into the sky.

"It's a summoning spell," the Fairy Queen murmured, her eyes wide. "But who is he summoning?"

The Fairy Queen didn't have to wait long for her question to be answered. Megan gasped as ten red, winged creatures swooped down towards Sorcero over the mountains, their leathery wings beating and smoke billowing from their nostrils. Dragons!

Before they could see any more, the image in the mirror became cloudy, then faded away. The Fairy Queen looked anxious. "The red dragons are good, noble creatures who live in the kingdom of Golden Spires and protect the people there," she said. "But they can cause terrible damage, too, with their fiery breath. And if Sorcero plans to use them

for his own ends, then the kingdom could be in grave danger."

Megan bit her lip, already afraid of what the beasts might do. In the past, Sorcero had seemed to think that by creating trouble, he could show himself to be a "hero" by rushing in and setting everything to rights once more. Was he plotting to do the same thing this time?

"Megan Andrews, what are you doing?" came her mum's voice again, followed by the sound of footsteps coming up the stairs.

"Quick! Send me into the kingdom of Golden Spires and I'll find out what's happening," Megan hissed.

"Thank you," the Fairy Queen replied. "All you need to do, is—"

But Megan knew what to do – and she

had to do it before her mum walked in! Her heart thumping, she touched the end of the Fairy Queen's wand. "Take me to the kingdom of Golden Spires!" she whispered urgently.

A flood of silver sparkles poured from the wand and swirled around Megan. Just as she heard her bedroom door begin to open, she felt herself being pulled away very fast, and everything blurred before her eyes. She was off on another magical adventure!

Chapter Two

Once the world had stopped spinning and her feet were on solid ground once more, Megan blinked and stared at her new surroundings. She was standing in a large, grand ballroom with polished floors, twinkling chandeliers and huge windows overlooking a flower-filled garden. "I must be in some kind of palace," she murmured.

Then she remembered to glance down at herself – because it wasn't only the world that changed when she travelled into the Land of Eight Kingdoms. She changed too!

This time, she was wearing a long turquoise dress with a tight bodice. On her feet were golden slippers, decorated with gleaming rubies. "I look like a princess!" Megan smiled. Then she remembered the reason she was here: to see what the dragons were up to. "I'd better get going," she decided.

Making her way across the ballroom, she heard raised voices and stopped to listen. "Absolutely not," a woman said. "Especially while the dragons are behaving so strangely. You must not ride alone, Paloma, and that's final."

Megan's ears pricked up. Dragons!

"But it's not fair, Mother," a second voice argued. "You know I'm an excellent rider, and I need to practise for the tournament this afternoon."

"And *you* know jolly well that I have

forbidden you to take part in the tournament," the woman replied crossly. "And I'm still furious that you entered the competition against my wishes. It's just not ladylike, Paloma. Princesses do not joust!"

Suddenly, the door in front of Megan was flung open and a girl marched through, her face set with impatience. Megan gulped when she saw the shining golden tiara on the girl's head and the long red dress she wore. She must be a princess!

"Hi," she said timidly, as the girl strode by. "Are you OK?"

The princess whirled round. "Who are you?" she asked.

"I'm Megan," replied Megan, slightly nervous of the way the princess was looking her up and down.

"Are you my new lady-in-waiting?" the princess asked briskly. "I hope you're going to last a bit longer than the other ones!"

Megan hesitated. She knew she couldn't tell anyone that she was helping the Fairy Queen in case word got back to Sorcero. "I… Yes, I hope so too," she said after a moment, remembering to drop a curtsey. "Your Highness," she added quickly.

Paloma looked amused. "You may call me Paloma," she said. "Let's go up to my chamber. I need to change for the joust, whatever my mother says. That's if it's still going ahead, of course. My parents have been threatening to call the whole thing off since the dragons attacked, worst luck."

Megan tried to take all of this in. A tournament, dragons, arguments with the Queen… There was certainly a lot going on! "These dragons … what exactly are they doing?" she asked.

Paloma looked surprised at the question.

"I've only just arrived in the Kingdom, you see," Megan added hastily. "I've been away for a while."

It wasn't a total lie – after all, she'd been away from the kingdom of Golden Spires for a very long time – her whole life, in fact!

Nonetheless, she felt uncomfortable that she wasn't being entirely truthful.

"Well, it's all very strange," Paloma replied, as they climbed a winding stone staircase. "The dragons live down in Rocky Valley, which is in the southern part of our kingdom, so we only see them twice a year. They come up north to light the autumn bonfires every year, and they always put on a fire show in the winter. But two

days ago, something peculiar happened."

They had reached the top of the staircase, and Paloma pushed open a wooden door. Megan followed her into a grand bedroom with a large four-poster bed draped in pink silk covers. The walls of the room were covered in prints of winged horses, and the windows were colourful stained glass. Megan could also see a vast wardrobe full of dresses and shoes.

"What a beautiful room," she said politely, as the princess flung her crown carelessly on the bed and kicked off her shoes.

"Thanks," said Paloma. "Anyway – the dragons. Yes. Two days ago, they appeared in the sky above the palace – and they were crying."

"Crying?" Megan echoed in surprise.

"Yes! Great scalding tears," Paloma said, pulling her dress off over her head and dumping it on the floor in a heap. "And that wasn't all." She was sorting through clothes in a drawer as she spoke, tossing out various pairs of trousers as she worked her way down. "I was out in the courtyard having the dreariest ever sketching lesson, but when the dragons saw me … well, they all divebombed me, basically. I had to sprint

indoors while poor old Mr Dray, my tutor, fainted clean away. Aha!" she cried, as she unearthed a pair of cream-coloured jodhpurs.

"Wow," said Megan, secretly impressed. The princess was being remarkably cool about what must have been a terrifying experience.

"Yes, it was all rather dramatic," Paloma said briskly, pulling on her jodhpurs. "Not only did the dragons' tears ruin Mother's precious rose garden, but she and Father are convinced that for some reason they made a direct attack on me." She wrinkled her nose. "Bet you're glad you're my lady-in-waiting now, aren't you? You probably didn't realize one of your duties might involve saving me from becoming a dragon's lunch!"

Chapter Three

"Wow," Megan said, her brain working quickly. Had Sorcero enchanted the dragons to attack the princess? Why had he made them cry? She wondered if he was hoping to scare or injure the royal family and their staff, and then turn up and pretend to save the day, as he'd tried before.

"What's strangest of all," Paloma went on, throwing on a purple polo shirt with a silver crown embroidered on it, "is that the Fairy Queen hasn't done anything about it. Not a thing! Usually she's

wonderful at sorting out this kind of problem – flies in, clears up any trouble, and on she goes. But she's not even popped in to see if we're OK – in fact, nobody's seen her in the kingdom for weeks now. Between you and me, my parents are rather miffed."

Megan felt awkward. She hated hearing the kind-hearted Fairy Queen criticized, especially as it was impossible to explain exactly why she hadn't appeared to help this time. "There must be a good reason why she hasn't come," she said after a moment.

"Hmmm," Paloma said darkly, checking her reflection in the mirror. Then she raised an eyebrow at Megan. "For a lady-in-waiting, you're not being very helpful," she said, casting a pointed

glance down at the clothes scattered across the floor.

Megan blushed. She'd forgotten she was supposed to be Paloma's servant! "Sorry," she said, bending down to scoop them up.

"You're not going to last long, I can tell," Paloma remarked, braiding her hair into a plait.

"Well, if you hadn't thrown your clothes everywhere, then—" Megan blurted out before she could stop herself. Then she clapped a hand to her mouth in horror. Oops! Some lady-in-waiting she was turning out to be!

Paloma looked astonished to be spoken to so rudely … but then, to Megan's relief, she actually grinned. "You're right," she said sheepishly. "Sorry. One gets so used to bossing other people around when one's a princess." She put her dress on a hanger and slotted it into the wardrobe, while Megan, still blushing, placed the golden crown on a red velvet cushion on the dressing table.

"Hey, I've got an idea," Paloma said, as she put on her riding helmet. "Why don't you come riding with me? I could do with a practice gallop to warm up for later."

"Well…" Megan hesitated. "I've never actually ridden a horse before," she confessed. "Not on my own anyway."

"Never ridden?" echoed Paloma, looking appalled. "Goodness! If you're

going to stick around with me, you'll have to learn. Here," she said, pulling out a riding outfit that was identical to hers. "Put these on. We're about the same size, so they should fit."

Megan changed into the jodhpurs and polo shirt, her heart galloping almost as fast as a horse. As she tied back her hair and put on the princess's spare riding hat, she caught Paloma staring at her. "Goodness – we look just the same now," the princess remarked. "We could be sisters!"

Megan grinned. "I always wanted a sister," she said.

"Me too," Paloma agreed with a smile. "Come on – I'll show you to the stables. We'll sneak out the back way so nobody spots us. This is going to be fun!"

The stables were in the far corner of the palace grounds, surrounded by rolling hills and flower-filled meadows. The air was fresh and fragrant, and the sky was clear of dragons, although Megan couldn't help glancing up nervously to check every few minutes. She was terrified of them attacking again, knowing that she'd have to protect the princess. What if she wasn't brave enough, and fainted in fright like Paloma's sketching tutor?

There were seven or eight winged horses in the stables, all hanging their

heads over the doors. When they glimpsed the princess approaching, several of them whickered with excitement and ruffled their thick feathery wings. Paloma looked just as delighted to see them and introduced them all to Megan. "This is Majesty," she said, stroking the gleaming silvery nose of the first horse. "And this is Celandine, and Florence, and Lottie, and Amber…"

One of the grooms came over. "Begging your pardon, Your Highness," he said uncertainly, "but the Queen gave us strict instructions that you weren't to go out riding on your own at the moment. So..."

Paloma gave him a brilliant smile. "Don't worry, Charlie," she said. "I won't be alone. This is Megan, my new bodyguard. She may look small, but she's a trained dragonslayer. They won't dare try anything with *her* by my side."

The groom gaped – and so did Megan. Bodyguard? Trained dragonslayer? Er … since when?

Paloma flashed her a pleading look, as if begging her to go along with the fib, so Megan nodded curtly to the groom. "I'll look after her," she declared.

"Very well," Charlie said, bowing low. "I'll saddle up Majesty and Celandine for you right away."

Paloma winked at Megan and it was all Megan could do not to burst into giggles. She'd never met anyone quite like Paloma before!

Once the horses had been saddled up, Megan took a deep breath and hauled herself on to Celandine, who was a gorgeous chestnut colour, with a gleaming golden mane and gold-tipped wings.

"Now, Celandine," Paloma said sternly, "Megan's never ridden on her own before so be gentle, all right?"

Celandine threw back her head and whinnied. It sounded worryingly like a laugh to Megan's ears.

"Let's go!" called Paloma, and Majesty, her horse, immediately broke into a trot. Moments later, Majesty's enormous wings unfolded and she lifted off the ground. Horse and rider were galloping through the air, Majesty's wings beating steadily.

Megan patted Celandine's glossy neck. "Let's do it," she said nervously. The horses didn't have bridles or reins, like they would do at a riding school back home, so Megan gripped hard with her knees and and clung on to Celandine's mane, hoping she could stay on.

Celandine trotted off, and Megan bounced up and down in her saddle. To her amazement, she didn't fall off. She was riding! But unfortunately, as soon as Celandine unfolded her magnificent wings and took off into the air, Megan completely lost her balance and slipped off sideways, landing with a bump on the soft grass. "Whoops," she laughed.

Celandine neighed in surprise, then turned in mid-air to land lightly next to Megan, nudging her with her velvety nose as if encouraging her to try again. But as hard as Megan tried to keep her balance in mid-air, she found it impossible. Riding

a flying horse was seriously difficult!

"Keep trying! You're doing well!" Paloma called out encouragingly, as she galloped through the air above.

Megan clambered back on to Celandine, trying not to think about how much her legs were aching. "This time I'll get it," she said, patting her horse apologetically. Paloma had vanished off into the distance, and Megan was determined to follow.

But once again, moments after Celandine took off, Megan found herself slithering helplessly off the horse's back and tumbling down to the ground.

"Oh dear," a mocking voice drawled, as she narrowly missed landing in a prickly bush. "Looks like you won't be winning the cup this year, Paloma. I might as well tell them to engrave my name on it now!"

Megan looked up to see a tall smirking boy astride a jet-black winged horse who reared up on its hind legs and whinnied. Before she could say anything, the horse had cantered off, with the boy shouting, "See you later, loser!" over his shoulder.

Megan stared after him. Who on earth was that? He'd obviously mistaken

her for Paloma, whoever he was.

Paloma galloped back to Megan a few moments later, and landed nearby. When Megan told her about the boy's taunts, the princess pulled a face. "I bet that was Tarquin Fotherington-Swine," she said crossly. "I can't stand him. He won the gold cup last year, but only because he cheated. I can't wait to see the look on his face when I beat him this time."

Just then, they heard the blare of trumpets in the distance. "Oh goodness!" Paloma exclaimed. "I had no idea it was so late. That's the call for the competitors to assemble at the tournament. Come on – we need to hurry!"

Chapter Four

It was only a short ride to the arena where the tournament was taking place, so they kept to the ground. To Megan's relief, she didn't fall off once. "Thank you, Celandine," Megan said gratefully, patting the horse's neck once she'd jumped down safely. Her first proper riding lesson had turned out to be one she'd never forget, that was for sure!

The arena was a large open space with seats built into the surrounding grassy banks. A crowd of people were already seated, waiting for the events to begin, and a band played jolly music on a small stage nearby. The King and Queen were waving to their citizens from the royal box, which was dressed in blue and gold. As soon as Paloma saw them, she grabbed Megan and dragged her out of sight, leading her and the horses to the stabling area.

There, other horses were being dressed in bright colours by their grooms. Everyone seemed busy, rushing here and there, some carrying long jousting poles, others with trays of steaming spiced drinks for the riders. A tall man in a long cloak jostled Megan as he went by and, for one heart-stopping moment, she thought it was Sorcero himself until Paloma told her it was only one of the event organizers.

"My event – the winged joust – is near the end of the tournament," Paloma said.

"It's the grand final joust – we've got through six heats, and only Tarquin and I are left competing. That's why I *have* to take part, no matter what Mother says." She glanced carelessly at the sky. "I mean, it's not like there are even any dragons around any more. I think it was just a one-off. A silly prank, that's all."

Megan glanced up at the sky too, feeling doubtful. If only she could believe that the dragons' attack really was a one-off. Knowing Sorcero, he'd keep attacking the royal family until he had reached his goal. But what *was* that?

"The grooms will give our horses something to eat and drink, then prepare Majesty for the joust, so we might as well watch for a while," Paloma said. "Look – I think the centaurs are going to race first."

Paloma and Megan sat down on a bench at the edge of the stable area where they had a perfect view of events, but could remain hidden from the King and Queen.

"Wow," Megan breathed as she saw six muscular centaurs take to the field. They had the bodies of horses, but human heads and chests. She'd only ever read about them in books before.

"Here we go," Paloma said, as a smartly dressed steward flung a handful of sparkling magic dust in the air. The dust glittered red, then amber, and then all of a sudden there was a flash of green light – the signal to go. Off galloped the centaurs, their faces determined as they thundered down the track, their powerful hooves kicking up clods of earth behind them.

The tallest centaur (whose horse body was a dusky grey) crossed the line first and threw back his head to shout in triumph. The audience erupted in applause.

"This is amazing," Megan said, bubbling with excitement.

Paloma grinned. "You wait, there's plenty more to come," she said. "What's next? Oh, the unicorn race – here they are!"

After the unicorn race, the steeplechase and a sword-fighting event, Megan's voice was hoarse from cheering. The tournament was the most thrilling thing she'd ever seen! Then a group of stewards threw colourful magic dust into the sky. It hung in mid-air to form a long line that stretched across the arena above everyone's heads.

"What's that?" asked Megan.

"The magical jousting rail, of course," Paloma replied, getting to her feet. "It must be my event next! You stay here, Megan, and I'll see you afterwards."

"Good luck," Megan called.

Paloma hurried off and Megan remained in her seat, looking forward to seeing her new friend compete. She knew from learning about knights in school that

jousting was the sport where two competing riders, divided by a rail, would gallop towards each other and try to knock one another off their horses with long lances. That would be nerve-racking enough to Megan – but presumably Paloma was going to joust in mid-air, which sounded even more terrifying! No wonder the Queen wasn't keen on her taking part.

"Ahh, here she is!" came a voice from behind her. "This way, Your Majesty, time for you to saddle up."

Megan turned to see two grooms, their heads bowed respectfully. How funny! They thought she was the princess too!

"Oh no, I'm not actually taking part—" she began, just as Tarquin went by.

"Has the princess got an attack of nerves?" he sneered. "Typical girl!"

Megan bristled. How dare he! During her adventures so far, she'd had to be smarter, tougher and braver than he'd ever be. She glared at him. "Girls are just as good as boys!" she retorted indignantly.

"A little respect for Her Highness, if you please," one of the grooms snapped at Tarquin, who rolled his eyes as if he didn't care. "Now, if Your Highness would like to come this way..." he went on, gesturing for her to follow.

"Ahh – the thing is ... you've made a mistake..." Megan tried to say.

Tarquin started making chicken noises. "Oh dear," he gloated. "The little *pwincess* is *fwightened*."

"You are so wrong," Megan said coldly, folding her arms across her chest. "Frightened of you? Never."

"Then what are you waiting for? Saddle up and let's see who's the best rider!" Tarquin challenged. "Unless you're worried that Mummy and Daddy might tell you off..."

This was more than Megan could bear. "You're the one who should be worried," she retorted. "Because you're going to feel such a fool when you lose!"

"You tell him, Your Highness," the second groom muttered approvingly as

Tarquin sauntered away. "Right, let's get you ready. I'm looking forward to seeing you beat him fair and square this year."

"Oh, but—" Megan said again. Help! The grooms were leading her to Majesty, who was wearing a special coat and head-dress in the royal colours of blue and gold. Before Megan could stop them, they were hoisting her up on to his back. "Wait!" she cried, but they were already leading her towards the area.

She stared around helplessly. Where on earth was Paloma? This was all going horribly wrong! "Excuse me!" she called out. "This is a mistake – I'm not the princess!"

The groom laughed. "Very funny, Your Highness," he said. "And I'm not a groom, neither. Best of luck to you." And with that, he patted Majesty's rear and the horse obediently trotted into the arena.

"And taking part in this year's jousting final, here is our first competitor, Her Royal Highness Princess Paloma!" announced a voice over a tannoy system. The band played a fanfare, and the audience stood up to applaud. Megan felt sick with nerves at having so many eyes on her. The King and Queen, meanwhile, looked utterly furious. Even *they* thought she was the princess! This was a disaster!

"Oh Majesty," she murmured, stroking the horse's soft silvery neck. "What are we going to do? I can't jump off you now, everyone will think Paloma has backed out of the contest."

Just as Megan was starting to despair, she heard a strange noise. It was a sort of

thrumming, quite faint at first as if it was coming from far away, but quickly becoming louder. Then everyone started screaming.

Megan stared upwards. Soaring towards her were three huge red dragons, their scaly wings beating through the sky. Just as Paloma had described before, sizzling hot tears were falling from their eyes.

"They're heading for the princess!" someone shouted. "Take cover, Your Highness. Quick!"

Frightened by the dragons, Majesty reared up on his hind legs and bolted, throwing Megan from his back. She landed awkwardly, but scrambled to her feet and began running blindly towards the nearest building – a stable. Seconds later though, she felt a tight grip on her back, and she was pulled up into the air. Megan screamed in terror to find herself dangling from the clawed feet of one of the dragons.

"The princess!" cried the crowd in horror. "The dragons are kidnapping the princess!"

Chapter Five

Megan was so frightened she could barely open her eyes as the dragon soared through the air at a dizzying height. She wasn't sure which was more scary – the thought of being dropped and plummeting to the ground, or the prospect of where they might be going. What if she was being taken directly to Sorcero? Had the horrible enchanter found out that she was the one who had been putting things to rights in the other kingdoms and spoiling his plans?

Soon the palace of Golden Spires was far behind, as the dragons flew across the

kingdom, tears falling all the while. Eventually, they reached a rocky valley and Megan was lowered to the ground. Dragons landed all around her.

Megan gazed about nervously. The valley was a desolate place surrounded by red boulders, making a quick escape look impossible. There were also enormous steaming puddles everywhere – some the size of small lakes – which must have been caused by the dragons' constant tears. They were still crying as they circled her, their breath hot on her face.

"W-Why have you brought me here?" she managed to say. She couldn't see any sign of Sorcero, but she knew he'd enchanted them and was wary of what he might have told them to do. Did dragons eat people?

Then, to her horror, Megan spotted even more dragons approaching, at least ten of them, all crying hot, fat tears. The largest dragon waved a clawed foot at a nearby rock that had some words carved into it. Megan moved closer and read them aloud.

Your tears will fall like scalding rain
Your hearts will ache with dreadful pain
Rivers will burst and floods will rise
Unless the princess can dry your eyes.

Megan's heart sank. This must be the enchantment that was binding the creatures – and it could only be broken by a princess. "But I'm not a princess," she said wretchedly. "I'm just Megan Andrews. I know I look like Princess Paloma, but I'm not actually her!"

The dragons went on weeping, tears streaming to the ground. There were new puddles all around them now, and the words of the carved message echoed in Megan's head. *Rivers will burst and floods will rise...* Was that Sorcero's plan? To flood the kingdom with dragon tears? At the rate the dragons were crying, it wouldn't take long to do so. And by commanding the dragons to snatch Princess Paloma, Sorcero must have known he'd throw the kingdom into a panic.

Megan's feet were becoming wet from the hot tears splashing around her. She might not be a princess, but surely there was a way she could stop them weeping...

"Come on, don't cry, it's all right," she said rather nervously to the nearest dragon. But his shoulders just shook with new sobs.

Megan bit her lip. Perhaps comforting words weren't enough. Sometimes when you were upset, you needed a hug too. Taking a deep breath, she unclipped her riding hat, then edged nearer the dragon and put her arm round his huge scaly neck. His skin felt hot and rough beneath her fingers as she patted it comfortingly. "There, there," she said in as soothing a voice as she could manage. "Don't worry, it'll be all right."

The dragon sniffled, then hiccupped. Then, to Megan's surprise, his tears stopped flowing altogether. Megan beamed. "That's better! How about a smile?"

The dragon bared its teeth in a rather watery smile and blew a little puff of black smoke from its nostrils.

"Well done!" Megan cried delightedly. "Now that I've cheered you up, let's see if I can do the same for one of your friends." She hurried along to the next dragon, no longer quite so frightened. "It's all right," she said soothingly, stroking his rough scales. "No need to cry. Don't worry."

After a few moments this dragon, too, stopped crying. Megan smiled. Hurrah!

Compared to the other challenges she'd faced in the Land of Eight Kingdoms, this one seemed almost too easy. She'd have cheered up all the dragons in no time.

But then she realized that the first dragon she'd comforted was already crying again, with new tears falling faster than ever. Moments later, the second dragon burst into fresh sobs too.

Megan's heart sank as she gazed around the group of weeping dragons. There were so many of them! How was she supposed to stop them all crying at once?

"Dragons, please! Tell me what's wrong!" she said desperately, but they just kept on weeping. And all the time, the puddles around her were getting bigger and bigger. What on earth was she going to do?

Chapter Six

Just then, Megan heard the beating of wings. She looked up to see a silvery horse galloping through the sky and relief washed over her. Swooping towards them was Princess Paloma on Majesty!

Majesty landed with a splash, and the princess leaped off her back. "Megan, are you all right?" she called, hurrying over. "I'm so sorry this has happened! I got locked in the bathroom. Then when I got out, I found the tournament in uproar, with everyone saying I'd been kidnapped. Only it was you instead!"

Megan had never been so glad to see a friendly face. "I'm OK," she said, hugging Paloma gratefully. "Thank you for coming to find me."

"There was no way I was going to leave you on your own," Paloma said. "Some friend I'd be! Mother was hugely relieved to see that it wasn't actually me who'd been kidnapped, and forbade me from following you, but I simply ignored her. I imagine they'll have sent the cavalry after me, but Majesty and I flew off before they could stop us." She wheeled round to address the weeping dragons. "I don't know what this is all about!" she said sternly. "But I'm shocked at your behaviour. Appalled! Has Tarquin put you up to this, or something? He'll do anything to try and beat me – well, it

won't work, I tell you. It simply will not!"

"I don't think they can stop themselves," Megan explained quickly as the dragons, looking upset at Paloma's words, cried harder than ever. "Read this." And she showed the princess the riddle that had been carved into the rock.

"Comforting the dragons works for a short time," she went on. "But then they just start crying again moments later. Maybe if you help me, we could—"

Paloma wasn't listening though. "If I've learned anything about being a princess it's that you need to be the boss," she said. "I shall just tell them to stop crying. If they know what's good for them, they'll obey." She put her hands on her hips, a determined glint in her eyes. "Dragons!" she shouted. "Be quiet immediately!"

The dragons flinched at her command, staring fearfully at Paloma. There was a split-second of silence before they all burst into noisy sobs once more. In fact, thought Megan, they seemed to be crying even louder and harder than ever.

Her shoes were soaked now, and the puddles were becoming uncomfortably hot, so she stepped up on to a rock that was still dry. "Your Highness, I don't think—" she faltered.

"DRAGONS!" Paloma thundered. "Stop this racket at once! I order you, by the Royal House of Cordaline to just … put a sock in it!"

The dragons merely kept weeping.

Princess Paloma looked flummoxed. "Oh," she said, staring at them. "How odd. Usually everyone does what I tell them to. And why aren't they saying anything? Usually they can speak perfectly normally."

"I think the enchantment means they can only cry," Megan said after a moment. She had to make the princess see that being bossy wasn't the right solution without offending her. Patting Majesty, who had gingerly stepped round the puddles to stand with them, Megan tried again. "Maybe we could…" she began.

But the princess was busily re-reading the riddle. "Aha!" she cried, interrupting Megan. "So that's it. The riddle says I have to dry their eyes. And look what I have in my pocket. Ta-dah!"

She pulled out a large white handkerchief, edged with gold thread, and with an embroidered crown in one corner. "A wipe with the royal handkerchief should do the trick," she declared, striding over to the nearest dragon. "There we are," she said briskly, as she dabbed away the tears. "You're done. Next!"

But no sooner had she dried one dragon's tears and moved on to another, than the first one started crying all over again. "Oh, for goodness' sake!" Paloma huffed in exasperation, staring at the weeping beasts. "What on earth's wrong with you?"

"I think they're under a powerful spell," Megan said, determined to be heard this time. "And we'll have to work together and think how to break it quickly before Rocky Valley turns into Rocky Lake."

"You're right," Paloma said. She nodded thoughtfully. "Working together!" she repeated, as if she'd never considered it before. "That might just be the answer." She tucked her soggy handkerchief in her pocket and walked back towards Megan.

"So what do you think we sh— Whooaa!"

Before she could finish her sentence, the princess slipped on a wet stone and splashed down into a puddle, spraying hot water everywhere. "Are you all right?" Megan asked, rushing over.

"I'm fine!" Paloma laughed. "Ooh, it's lovely and warm," she said, pretending to soap underneath her arms. "Just like a bath!"

Megan laughed too. The princess did look funny, wet-through.

Then she noticed that she and Paloma weren't the only ones who thought it was funny. Some of the dragons were giggling

as well. She stared as she saw little puffs of smoke coming from their nostrils. Had they … had they actually stopped crying?

Not quite. Moments later, the creatures had all burst into tears again.

An idea popped into Megan's head as she helped the princess to her feet. "Did you see that?" she asked. "Some of the dragons giggled when you fell over, and stopped crying for a little while. If we could make them all laugh at once, then maybe…"

"Maybe we could break the spell!" Paloma cried, her eyes sparkling. "Good idea. Quick – let's both do some more funny things. Do you know any jokes?"

Megan scratched her head. "What do you get when a dragon sneezes?" she asked after a moment. "Out of the way!"

Some of the dragons tittered politely, but others didn't seem amused and went on crying.

Paloma tried next. "What did the dragon say when he saw a knight in armour?" she asked. "Tinned food!"

Again, there were a few giggles, but some of the dragons were still weeping.

Megan thought hard. The dragons seemed to find it funniest when Paloma had fallen over. Maybe more clowning around was the answer? She picked up some small rocks and began juggling them, and Paloma jumped into another puddle, getting completely drenched. Even Majesty seemed to get the idea and performed a silly horse-dance, splashing around in circles.

The dragons giggled as Megan raced to

catch one of her rocks and skidded into a pool of water.

They chuckled as Paloma did a handstand in the puddle and emerged with her hair dripping wet.

And they roared with laughter when Majesty got on his back legs and pretended to walk like Paloma.

Megan held her breath as the dragons went on laughing and laughing. Had the plan actually worked?

Chapter Seven

Suddenly the air crackled with magic, and there was a bright flash of purple sparks all around the dragons. Megan crossed her fingers excitedly. She'd seen similar magical reactions in the past, when Sorcero's other enchantments had been broken. But had they broken this one too?

Then, one by one, the dragons began puffing smoke through their nostrils. The biggest dragon opened his mouth and roared out a jet of bright orange flames, his eyes sparkling with happiness.

"Bravo, Your Highnesses, bravo!" he cheered in a deep, scratchy voice, then soared up into the air and did a loop the loop. The other dragons cheered, and all began talking joyfully at once. Soon they were flying around in a circle together looking a hundred times happier.

Megan hugged Paloma. "We did it!" she cried. "We broke the enchantment!"

Paloma hugged her back. "All thanks to you," she said warmly. The girls drew apart and the princess added thoughtfully, "I mean it. I'm so used to getting everything I want, when I want it, that it wouldn't have occurred to me to work together, let alone make them laugh. We couldn't have freed them without your brilliant idea, Megan."

"We make a good team," Megan said with a grin. "And now we'd better get back to the tournament. Haven't you got a cup to win?"

Paloma brightened. "I so have!" she replied.

Just then, they heard the beating of wings and saw the cavalry galloping in, their winged horses making a dark cloud in the sky. Paloma rolled her eyes. "Some help they were!" she said to Megan.

"Who needs the army when you've got a clever friend, eh?"

Megan beamed and felt tingly all over. She was glad to be friends with Princess Paloma!

The soldiers landed a safe distance from the dragons and eyed them nervously. "Don't worry about us, we're fine," Paloma called out dryly. "We'll be back at the palace once we've said our goodbyes."

The dragons floated down to land just then, and the largest one spoke. "A thousand thank yous," he said, bowing his head. "Oh, it's good to be able to speak again! I feel as if I have just woken from the strangest, saddest dream."

Megan stroked his scaly nose. "Well now you are free once more," she told him.

The dragon bowed his head again.

"Thank you," he said simply. "Please allow us to escort you back to the palace."

Megan and Paloma exchanged smiles of delight. "A dragon escort would be wonderful!" Megan said.

Megan clipped her riding hat back on, then she and Paloma sat astride Majesty's back and the graceful horse took off into the sky, its powerful wings taking them swiftly and smoothly through the air. The dragons followed, arranging themselves in an arrow-shaped formation around Majesty, with the cavalry flying behind. It must have been quite a sight from the ground, Megan thought, feeling thrilled as she clung on to Paloma's waist. And it was certainly a far more enjoyable flight than the one she'd had earlier, dangling from a dragon's claws!

After a while she saw the gleaming spires and turrets of the palace in the distance, and minutes later she and Paloma landed in the arena to a heroes' welcome. Everyone was on their feet, clapping, cheering and whistling. The King and

Queen rushed out from the royal box and flung their arms round Paloma in relief. "Are you all right? Are you hurt?" asked the Queen.

Paloma shook her head. "The dragons were under a spell," she explained. "They couldn't stop crying, and only a princess could break the enchantment. And that's what we – my friend and I – did."

"Your daughter and her friend showed true courage and quick thinking," the largest of the dragons declared. "And they know some excellent jokes too," he added, winking at Paloma and Megan.

"We are sorry we scared you earlier," a second dragon said, addressing the crowd. "Please believe us when we say we'd never hurt any of you. The enchantment caused us to act against our will."

"Hooray for Princess Paloma and her noble friend!" the crowd cheered. "Hooray for the dragons!"

"Well done, girls," the King said gravely. "You have been extremely courageous. And as for you poor dragons – tell us who did this to you and they shall be punished."

The largest dragon scratched his head with a claw. "That's the strange thing, Your Highness," he replied in his low, throaty rumble. "None of us can remember. It's a complete blank."

"Whoever cast such an enchantment must have used powerful magic," the

queen said, frowning. She turned to her husband. "You don't think it could have been the Fairy Queen, do you? After all, nobody has seen her for weeks."

"It wasn't the Fairy Queen!" Megan blurted out. Then she blushed as everyone stared at her. Oh no. So much for keeping secret what she knew!

Luckily, the dragon spoke again. "The Fairy Queen is a friend to all dragons," he said. "We're certain she would not use bad magic against us."

"Well, we'll get to the bottom of this, mark my words," the King said. "But right now, I believe there's one last event left of our tournament ... and then there will be a great banquet in honour of Paloma and her friend. So, dearest Paloma, if you still want to take part in the joust...?"

Princess Paloma's face lit up. "Really? You're happy for me to joust against Tarquin? Even though it's not ladylike?"

The queen laughed. "After your heroism today, Paloma, you've more than proved your bravery and loyalty. Those qualities are far more important than being ladylike." She lowered her voice. "Just make sure you beat that little creep Tarquin. I gather he's been boasting all day that he's going to win the cup."

Paloma grinned. "Leave it to me, Mother," she said.

Megan sat with the King and Queen in the Royal Box to watch the joust. When Princess Paloma knocked Tarquin off his winged horse with the very first thrust

of her lance, Megan thought she might be deafened by the delighted roar from the entire audience. She jumped to her feet too, cheering proudly for the spirited princess. *Score one to the girls,* she thought with a smile, as Tarquin slunk away in a gigantic sulk.

Afterwards, there was a huge party back at the palace with dancing and a great feast. As the sky darkened, the dragons lit an enormous bonfire so that everyone could toast marshmallows, then performed a stunning fiery aerobatic display.

Megan and Paloma stood together in the garden, oohing and ahhing as the dragons nimbly flipped and spun above their heads. And then, just as Megan was wishing her adventure in the kingdom of Golden Spires would never end, she heard the tinkling melody from the music box ringing in her ears, and knew her time was almost up.

"I've got to go," she told Paloma, "but I just want to say how much fun I've had. Thanks for a great day."

"What do you mean?" Paloma asked, startled. "You're going? But I thought we were friends!"

Megan grabbed her hand and squeezed it. "We *are* friends," she promised. "But I can't stay … and I'm afraid I can't explain why. I'm not from here and I have to go home, that's all I can say."

The music was getting louder and Megan could hardly hear Paloma's reply. "But when will you come back?"

"I don't know. I'm sorry, but I've got to go. Goodbye!"

"Goodbye!" Megan heard Paloma shout as she ran out of the garden. Megan had just ducked behind a hedge when she felt herself being lifted off her feet by the magic and spun around. In the next moment, the kingdom of Golden Spires vanished in a blur of coloured light.

Chapter Eight

Megan felt herself rushing along very fast, dazzled by the bright lights all around her. Finally, the world seemed to swing round one last time, and then she was back in her bedroom. Seconds later, the door opened and her mum appeared.

"There you are! Come on – we're going to be late," Mrs Andrews said. "What's kept you so long? You're not nervous about your riding lesson, are you?"

Megan hid her smile. Nervous about riding a pony, after she'd ridden a winged

horse in the kingdom of Golden Spires? No chance! "I'm looking forward to it," she replied. "I'll be down in one minute."

Her mum left the room and Megan's eyes lit up as she saw a shiny new treasure in her music box. It was a silver charm in the shape of a horseshoe!

The Fairy Queen was smiling at her. "So … how was your adventure? What had Sorcero done this time?" she whispered.

As quickly as she could, Megan explained about Princess Paloma and the dragons, and the enchantment Sorcero had cast upon them.

"What an exciting adventure!" the Fairy Queen cried. "And your bravery and kindness to a new friend mean that Sorcero's enchantment on me has been weakened also. Look!"

To Megan's delight, the Fairy Queen raised both arms above her head and fluttered them joyfully down again.

"Hooray," Megan cheered. "That's the best news of all. Just four kingdoms left to visit – and then you will be free!"

The Fairy Queen looked wistful. "Oh, Megan, I hope so," she said. "I am longing to return home to see my friends once more. I miss them terribly." Her face fell as the music began to slow. "But now I fear my magic is draining away and I must leave you until the next time," she said. The brightness in her eyes began to dim, and the pink of her cheeks paled.

"Thank you, Megan. Goodbye for now!"

"Goodbye," Megan whispered, as the Fairy Queen froze. Then she hurried out of her bedroom and down the stairs, smiling to herself. She really was the luckiest girl in the world. And who would she meet on her next adventure? She couldn't wait to find out!

Epilogue

"I don't believe it. I simply don't believe it!" With a roar of rage, Sorcero thumped his hand down on the table in his spell-chamber. "How did Princess Paloma manage to break my enchantment on the dragons? I was sure she'd be too impatient to work it out. The kingdom was supposed to be on the brink of ruin, before I swooped in to the rescue."

He kicked out at a wooden stool, sending it crashing to the stone floor.

"Someone must have helped her, someone with magic powers," he decided. "But who?"

He stamped around the spell-chamber, a dreadful frown deepening the lines on his forehead. "I can't give up now," he

muttered angrily. "The question is, what do I do next?"

He grabbed his magic magnifying glass and went back to the table, leaning over the large map that lay there. By moving the glass over the different kingdoms, he could see what was happening in each place. After a few moments, Sorcero scratched his head thoughtfully. "I wonder if..." he mused. "Yes, that's a very good idea, even if I do say so myself. And this time my enchantment will prove impossible to break!"